Curious George®

AT THE BEACH

Adapted from the Curious George film series
edited by Margret Rey and Alan J. Shalleck

1 9 8 8

Houghton Mifflin Company, Boston

Library of Congress Cataloging-in-Publication Data

Curious George at the beach/edited by Margret Rey and Alan J. Shalleck.
    p. cm.
  "Adapted from the Curious George film series."
  Summary: Curious George's natural agility gives him an unfair
advantage when he joins a volleyball game at the beach, but it also
helps him rescue a little boy who almost falls off a pier.
  ISBN 0-395-48666-1
  [1. Beaches—Fiction. 2. Monkeys—Fiction.] I. Rey, Margret.
II. Shalleck, Alan J. III. Curious George at the beach (Motion picture)
PZ7.C92128   1988   88-12268
[E]—dc19   CIP
               AC

Printed in the United States of America

Y   10 9 8 7 6 5 4 3 2 1

"It's very warm today, George,"
said the man with the yellow hat.
"Let's go to the beach."

The beach was very crowded on such a hot day.

"I'm going to change into my trunks," said the man.
"Look around, but don't get into trouble, George."

George started to explore.
Someone had built a castle in the sand.

People were splashing and swimming in the water.

Nearby, a group of boys and girls
were playing volleyball.

George wanted to play too, but no one seemed to notice.

So he climbed up onto the net, and
when the ball came his way, he grabbed it. What fun!

George jumped over the heads of the players
and landed on the sand.
Now he could play with them.

"Hey!" someone shouted. "Give us back the ball!"

Then the players chased George. He was scared.
He dropped the ball and ran away.

Now where could he go?

Then he saw a lifeguard tower.

While the lifeguard was pulling his boat
out of the water,
George climbed onto the tower.

George could see a lot from up here!

George picked up the lifeguard's binoculars
and looked through them.

Everything seemed so close!
He could see a little boy on the pier.

Nearby, a woman was sleeping in a beach chair.

George looked at the boy again.
Now the boy was running.

He was running straight toward a hole in the pier.
He could fall through!

George blew the lifeguard's whistle.

Then he jumped down and ran to the pier.

George reached the boy
just as he was about to fall.

George grabbed him.

Meanwhile, the lifeguard had heard the whistle
and ran over to help them.

Then George's friend and the woman
who had been sleeping   rushed over too.

"If it wasn't for you," the lifeguard said to George,
"this little boy would have been in real trouble."

The woman gave George a big hug.
"Thank you," she said. "You saved my grandson's life."

She turned to George's friend.
"Won't you both have something to eat with us?"

So they all had lunch on the beach.
"A hero deserves a good meal," said the woman.
George agreed.